Garfield®
GARZILLA
BY JIM DAVIS

GARFIELD: GARZILLA, March 2020. Published by KaBOOM!, a division of Boom Entertainment, Inc.

BOOM! Studios, 5670 Wilshire Boulevard, Suite 400, Los Angeles, CA 90036-5679. Printed in China. First Printing.

ISBN: 978-1-68415-497-5, eISBN: 978-1-64144-655-6

CONTENTS

COVER BY ANDY HIRSCH

DESIGNER CHELSEA ROBERTS
EDITOR CHRIS ROSA

GARFIELD CREATED BY
JIM DAVIS

SPECIAL THANKS TO JIM DAVIS AND THE ENTIRE PAWS, INC. TEAM.

TRA

"GARZILLA"

BOOM BOOM
BOOM BOOM
BOOM BOOM
BOOM BOOM
OH, MY...
LOOK!
MARKET

GARZILLA
RROWW
RR

THIRTY-SIX HOURS EARLIER...
Dr. Lyndsey Lee. Experiment X95-43J notes. Day 14. I've isolated the protein compound...
...and run the sequence multiple times. The protein is stable and ready for the next step.
I am preparing the subject for introduction.
GOOD MORNING, TESLA...
squee squee
L94
Subject L94, a.k.a. "Tesla." Rattus norvegicus, age three years, seven months. Subject suffers from age-related organ failure.
Previous subjects have rejected the protein. Newest modifications to protein hopefully will be accepted.
SQUEAK?

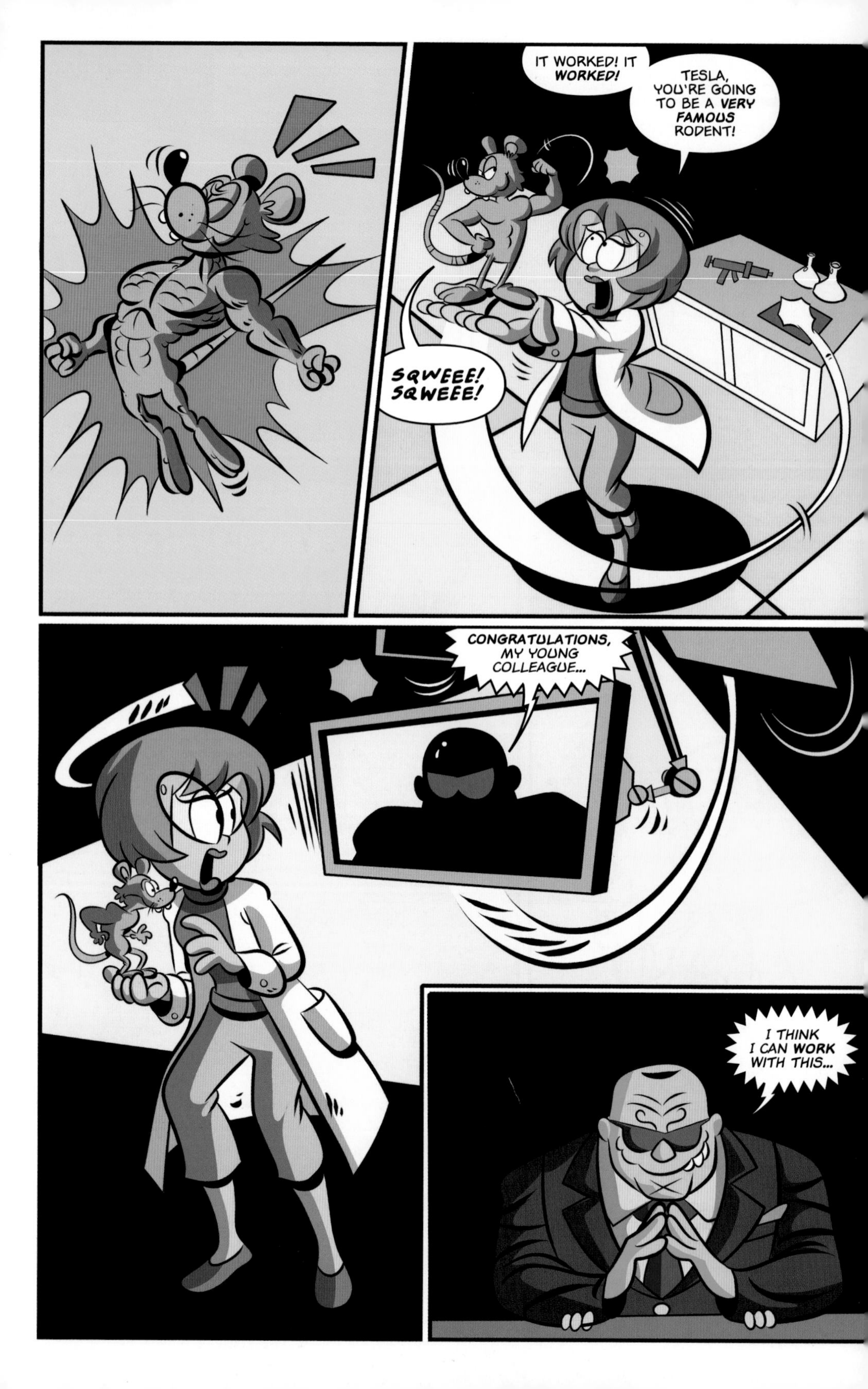
IT WORKED! IT WORKED!
TESLA, YOU'RE GOING TO BE A VERY FAMOUS RODENT!
SQWEEE! SQWEEE!
CONGRATULATIONS, MY YOUNG COLLEAGUE...
I THINK I CAN WORK WITH THIS...

GULP CHEW GOBBLE SNORF MUNCH
GARFIELD!
YOU'LL SPOIL YOUR APPETITE FOR VITO'S PIZZA!
I'M NOT SPOILING MY APPETITE. I'M JUST WARMING IT UP.
BRING ON THE PIZZA, MY HAPLESS-YET-LOVEABLE OWNER!

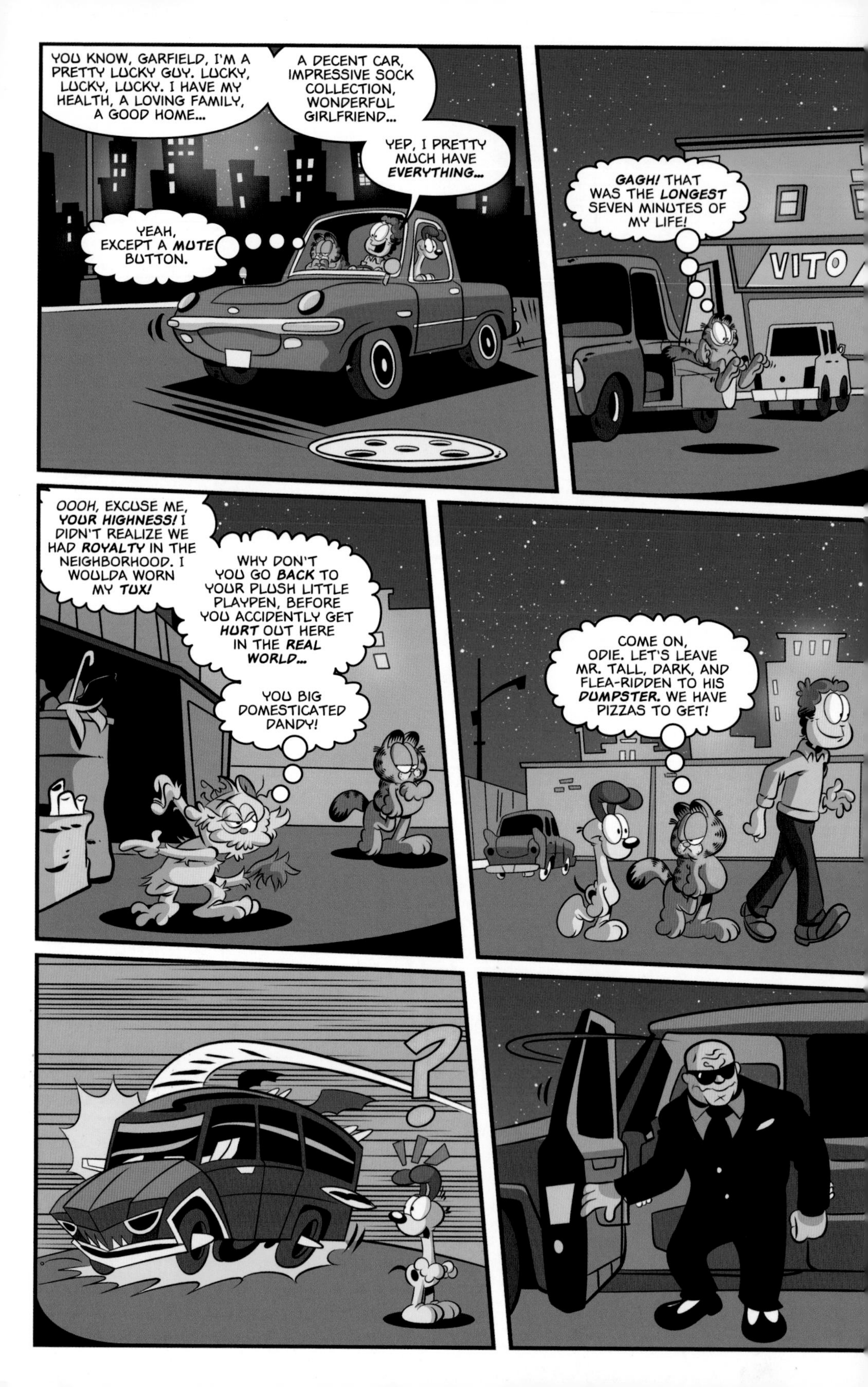
YOU KNOW, GARFIELD, I'M A PRETTY LUCKY GUY. LUCKY, LUCKY, LUCKY. I HAVE MY HEALTH, A LOVING FAMILY, A GOOD HOME...
A DECENT CAR, IMPRESSIVE SOCK COLLECTION, WONDERFUL GIRLFRIEND...
YEP, I PRETTY MUCH HAVE EVERYTHING...
YEAH, EXCEPT A MUTE BUTTON.
GAGH! THAT WAS THE LONGEST SEVEN MINUTES OF MY LIFE!
VITO
OOOH, EXCUSE ME, YOUR HIGHNESS! I DIDN'T REALIZE WE HAD ROYALTY IN THE NEIGHBORHOOD. I WOULDA WORN MY TUX!
WHY DON'T YOU GO BACK TO YOUR PLUSH LITTLE PLAYPEN, BEFORE YOU ACCIDENTLY GET HURT OUT HERE IN THE REAL WORLD...
YOU BIG DOMESTICATED DANDY!
COME ON, ODIE. LET'S LEAVE MR. TALL, DARK, AND FLEA-RIDDEN TO HIS DUMPSTER. WE HAVE PIZZAS TO GET!
?

HERE, KITTY, KITTY...
HEY, WHAT GIVES? IS THIS SOME KIND OF TRICK?
YOU'RE PROBABLY FROM ANIMAL CONTROL, JUST WAITIN' TO NAB ME.
IT'S OKAY, KITTY. DON'T YOU WANT THE FOOD?
IT'S FANCY ALBACORE...
FANCY ALBACORE TUNA? THAT'S WHAT RICH KITTIES GET. HEY, MAYBE THIS IS MY TICKET TO THE SWEET CUSHY LIFE!
GOT YOU!
CLANG
BARK! BARK!

BARK! BARK! BARKITTY BARK!
WHIIINE...
BARK! BARK! BARK!
YOU SAW WHAT?! A MAN GAVE THAT ALLEY CAT SOME FOOD AND THEN TOOK HIM AWAY IN A CARRIER?
SO LOUIE FINALLY FOUND A HOME. BIG DEAL.
BARK! BARK! BARK!
HE WAS EVIL? HOW DO YOU KNOW THAT? ANYONE WHO OFFERS SOLID WHITE ALBACORE TUNA TO A DIRTY ALLEY CAT IS NOT EVIL.
FISCALLY IRRESPONSIBLE, MAYBE, BUT NOT EVIL.

WE ARE NOT GOING TO CHASE AFTER THAT CAR. THE CAT IS FINE, AND I HAVE SEVERAL LARGE PIZZAS TO CONSUME.
WHIIINE
HOW ABOUT A LITTLE MORE TUNA, EH, KITTY, KITTY?
THIS DOESN'T LOOK VERY SOFT AND PLUSHY, BUT WHO CAN TURN DOWN ALBACORE?
THRUMMMMMM
THRUMMM
?!
SNAKKT
NOW WE HAVE YOU SAFE AND SNUG, MY FELINE FRIEND.

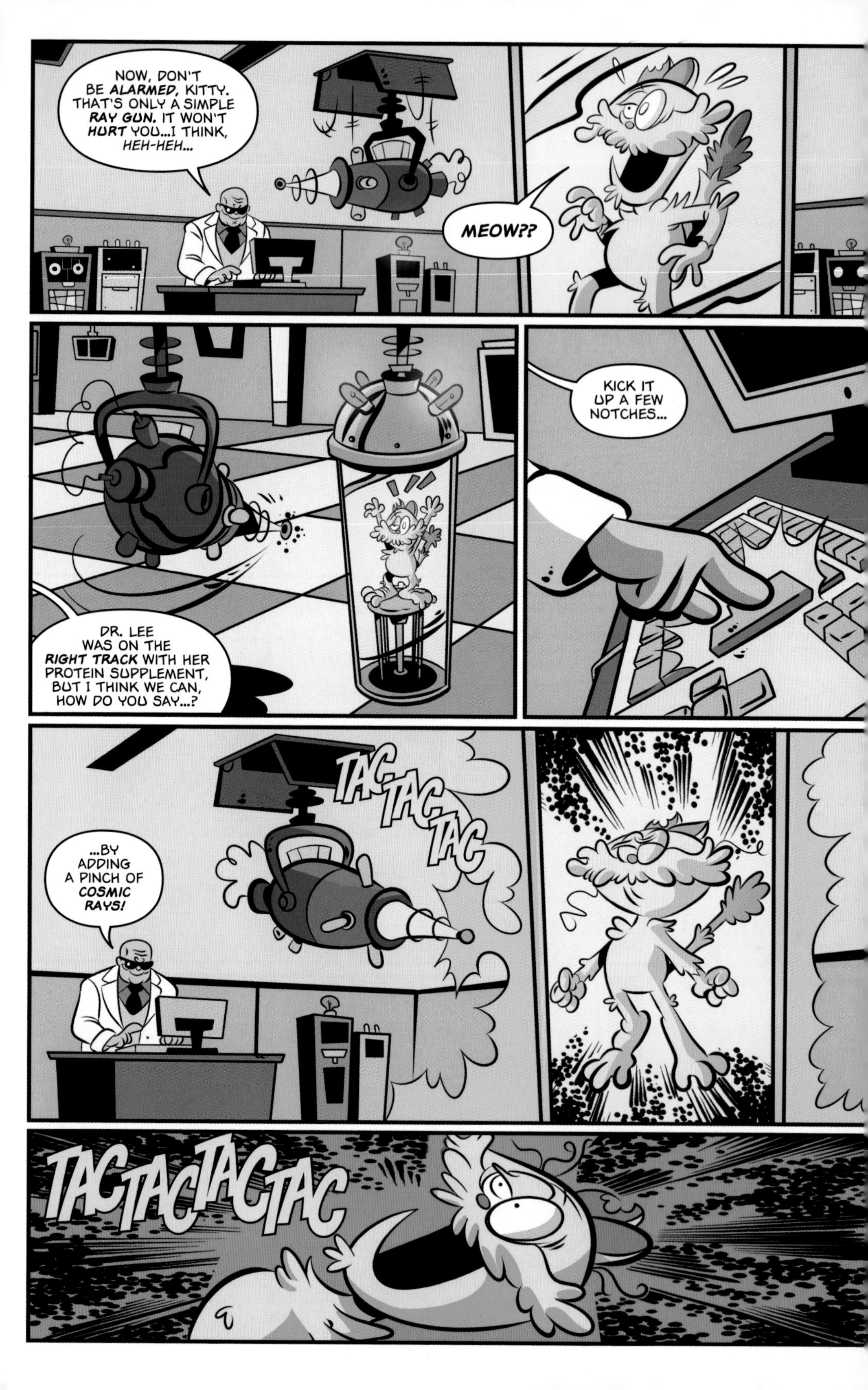
NOW, DON'T BE ALARMED, KITTY. THAT'S ONLY A SIMPLE RAY GUN. IT WON'T HURT YOU...I THINK, HEH-HEH...
MEOW??
DR. LEE WAS ON THE RIGHT TRACK WITH HER PROTEIN SUPPLEMENT, BUT I THINK WE CAN, HOW DO YOU SAY...?
KICK IT UP A FEW NOTCHES...
...BY ADDING A PINCH OF COSMIC RAYS!
TAC TAC TAC
TACTACTACTACTAC

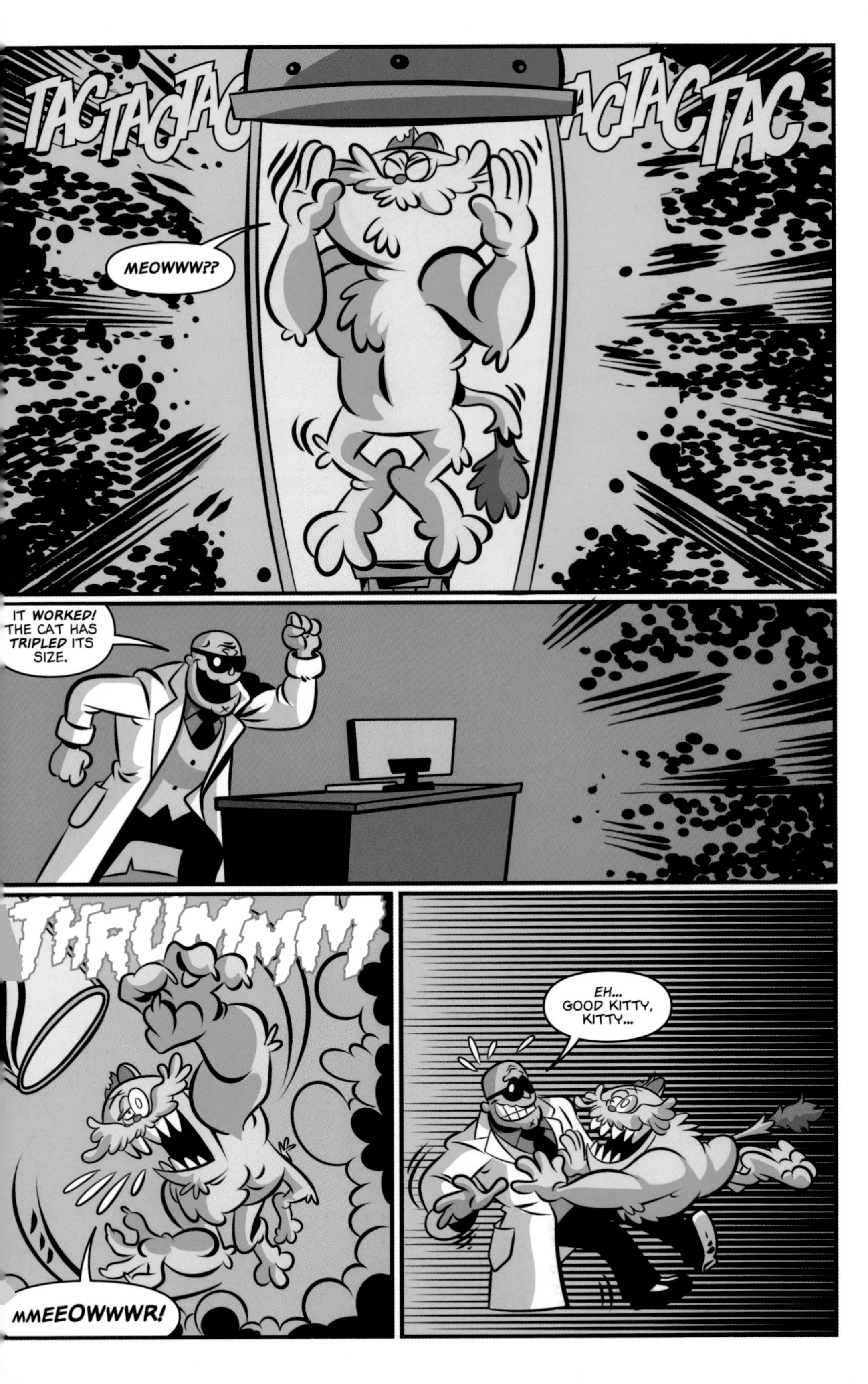
TACTACTACTAC
TACTACTACTAC
MEOWWW??
IT WORKED! THE CAT HAS TRIPLED ITS SIZE.
THRUMMM
MMEEOWWWR!
EH... GOOD KITTY, KITTY...

MEEEOOWWWRRR??
OOOF!
HOW ABOUT SOME MORE FOOD?
LACED WITH A SEDATIVE TO KEEP YOU UNDER CONTROL, OF COURSE.
MOMENTS LATER...
THE PROCESS WORKED, BUT IF I'M GOING TO SELL THIS TECHNOLOGY TO A FOREIGN GOVERNMENT, I NEED SOMETHING A LITTLE MORE SPECTACULAR...
BARK! BARK!
?
BARK BARK BARK!
WHY, HELLO, PUPPY...

THIRTY MINUTES EARLIER...
OKAY, SO THAT'S THREE LARGE PEPPERONI, TWO LARGE HAWAIIAN WITH PINEAPPLE AND HAM, ONE MAMMOTH MEATY SUPREME, ONE SUPER-DUPER SUPREME, FOUR ORDERS OF LASAGNA, CHEESY GARLIC BREAD, AND A SMALL SIDE SALAD WITH FAT-FREE ITALIAN DRESSING.
THAT'S FOR *LIZ.*
GOOD. MORE PIZZA AND PASTA FOR *ME!*
IT WAS NICE OF VITO TO THROW IN AN *EXTRA ORDER OF BREAD STICKS!*
VITO IS THE *MAN!*
HEY, WAIT A MINUTE. WHERE'S *ODIE?*

THAT'S RIGHT, BOY. GOBBLE DOWN THAT PROTEIN SUPPLEMENT-INFUSED KIBBLE!
MUNCH
GOBBLE
SNORT
I'VE RESET THE COORDINATES, INCREASING THE LEVEL OF COSMIC RAYS. IF MY CALCULATIONS ARE CORRECT, THE RESULTS WILL BE MOST IMPRESSIVE.
THRUMMMMM
THRUMMMMM
HUH?
SNAKKT
IT'S SHOW TIME, FOLKS!
MAX

TACTACTACTAC
TACTAC
TAC
THERE! THAT SHOULD DO IT.
WAIT, SOMETHING'S **WRONG.** HE'S NOT **GROWING.**
THRUMMMMMM

AH, GOOD. NOW IT'S WORKING. I WAS AFRAID MY CALCULATIONS WERE OFF...
BARK BARK BARK!
WHAM
WHIIINE
OH, MY!

EEP
EXPERIMENT NOTES: MY CALCULATIONS FOR INCREASED COSMIC RAY OUTPUT WERE INDEED CORRECT. THE DOG IS AT LEAST THIRTY-FIVE-FEET TALL.
SUBJECT WILL BE KEPT IN AN EMPTY WAREHOUSE NEXT TO THE LAB.
I DO HOPE HE'S HOUSEBROKEN!

HOWWWWLLLLLLL
ODIE? ODIE?
THAT DOPEY DOG! WHILE HE'S WHO KNOWS WHERE, MY PIZZA IS GETTING COLD!
HOWWWWLLLLLLL
WHAT WAS THAT?
I DON'T KNOW, AND I DON'T WANT TO KNOW!
BOOM BOOM BOOM
IS THAT AN EARTHQUAKE? DO WE GET EARTHQUAKES IN INDIANA?
WHATEVER IT IS, IT'S GETTING CLOSER!

SPLASH!
DO WE GET TSUNAMIS IN INDIANA, TOO?
WHAT WAS THAT?!
GARFIELD! LOOK! IT'S...
ODIE!
GIGANTIC ODIE...
YEAH, AND WE'RE STANDING IN GIGANTIC ODIE DROOL, TOO!
YUCK! YUCK! AND DOUBLE YUCK!

ODIE... H-HOW DID YOU GET SO...SO... GINORMOUS?!
ARF
ARF!
AGHH! THAT SOUND-- DEAFENING!
DON'T BARK, ODIE. JUST NOD YOUR HEAD.
YIP!
BOOM
BOOM
BOOM

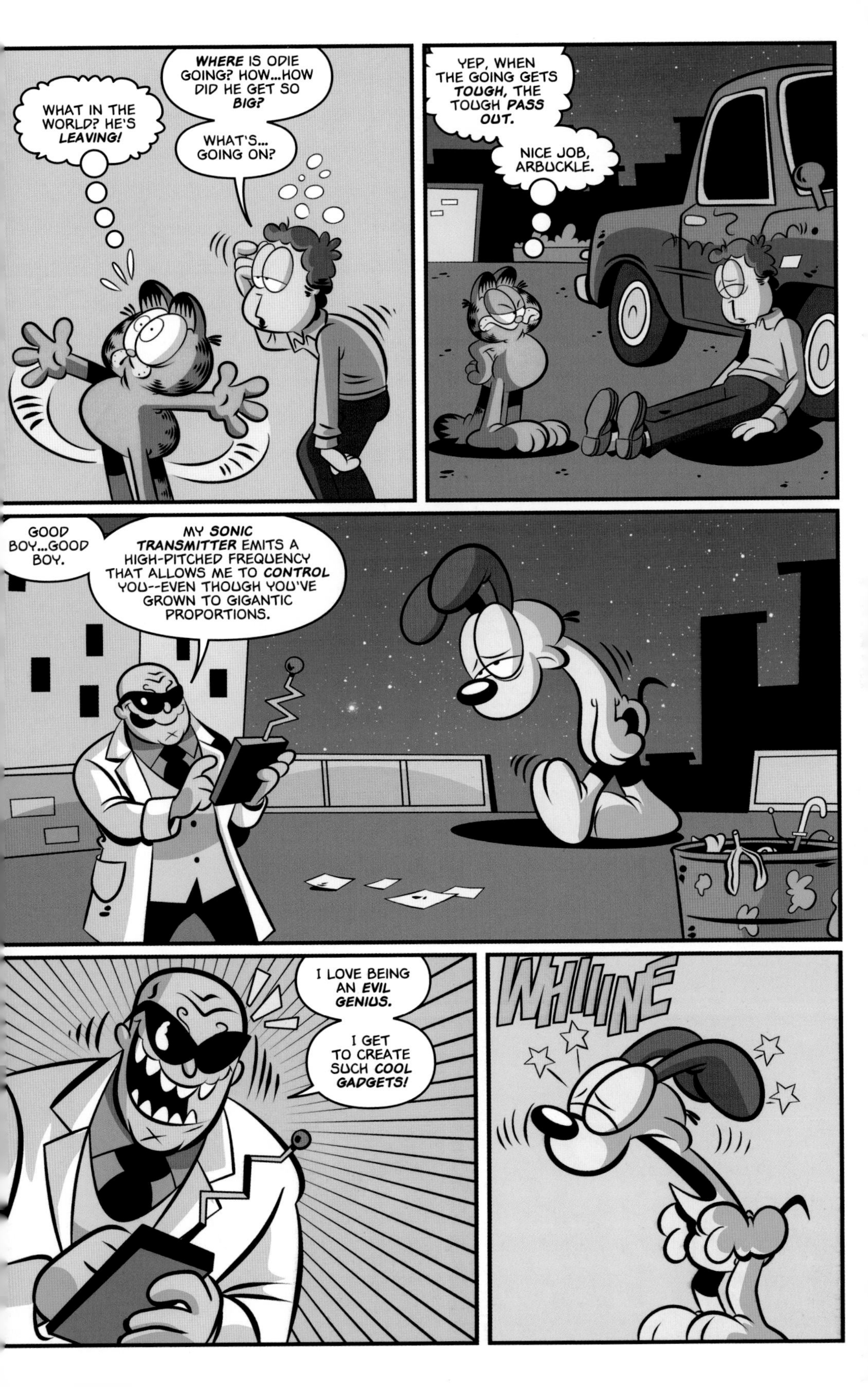
WHAT IN THE WORLD? HE'S LEAVING!
WHERE IS ODIE GOING? HOW...HOW DID HE GET SO BIG?
WHAT'S... GOING ON?
YEP, WHEN THE GOING GETS TOUGH, THE TOUGH PASS OUT.
NICE JOB, ARBUCKLE.
GOOD BOY...GOOD BOY.
MY SONIC TRANSMITTER EMITS A HIGH-PITCHED FREQUENCY THAT ALLOWS ME TO CONTROL YOU--EVEN THOUGH YOU'VE GROWN TO GIGANTIC PROPORTIONS.
I LOVE BEING AN EVIL GENIUS.
I GET TO CREATE SUCH COOL GADGETS!
WHIIINE

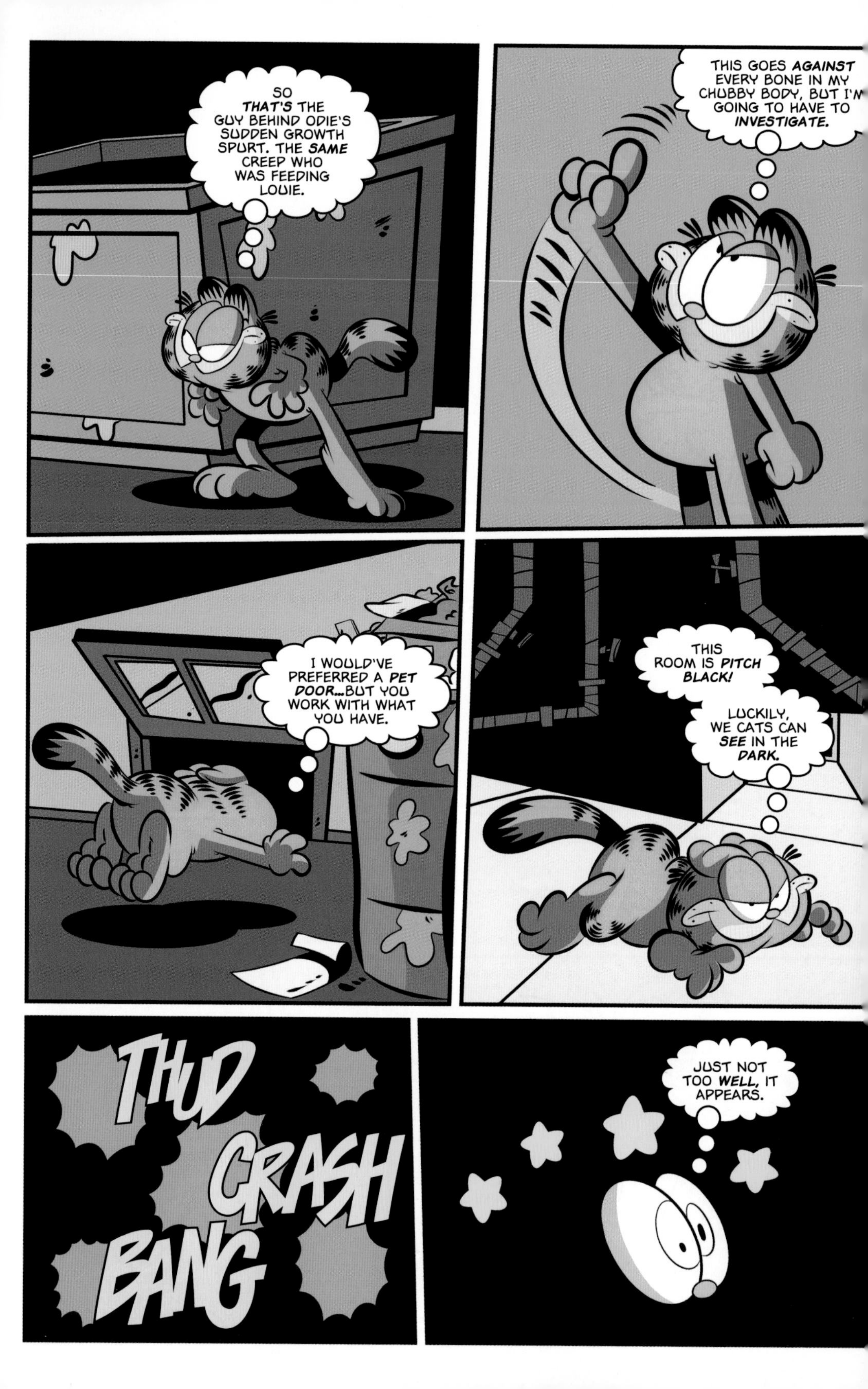
SO THAT'S THE GUY BEHIND ODIE'S SUDDEN GROWTH SPURT. THE SAME CREEP WHO WAS FEEDING LOUIE.
THIS GOES AGAINST EVERY BONE IN MY CHUBBY BODY, BUT I'M GOING TO HAVE TO INVESTIGATE.
I WOULD'VE PREFERRED A PET DOOR...BUT YOU WORK WITH WHAT YOU HAVE.
THIS ROOM IS PITCH BLACK!
LUCKILY, WE CATS CAN SEE IN THE DARK.
THUD
CRASH
BANG
JUST NOT TOO WELL, IT APPEARS.

!?!
IT APPEARS WE HAVE COMPANY. HELLO, CAT.
GULP!
IT SEEMS THE FATES HAVE SMILED ON ME TONIGHT. SUCH AN EMBARRASSMENT OF RICHES.
NOT ONE, NOT TWO, BUT THREE SUBJECTS FOR MY EXPERIMENT! I'M GIDDY LIKE A SCHOOL BOY.
SUBJECTS FOR YOUR EXPERIMENT?! THINK AGAIN, DR. DOOFUS. I'M HERE TO BRING ODIE HOME.
EAH, BIG GIANT ODIE. HOW'S THIS GOING TO WORK?
HOW ABOUT A LITTLE SNACK?
IT'S ALBACORE TUNA.
YUMMY, YUMMY!

MEOWWRR!
I'LL PLAY ALONG. BUT DON'T WORRY, COMIC BOOK READERS, I HAVE A PLAN!
OOH, TUNA! MY FAVORITE.
GOBBLE
SNARF
GULP
THRUMMMMMM
THAT'S RIGHT, DR. EVIL DUDE... LOCK ME IN...
MAX
NOW TO ADJUST THE RAYS' OUTPUT EVEN HIGHER.

THEN EVEN HIGHER THAN THAT!
MUHAHAHAHA!
MAX PLUS
AN EVIL SUPER-VILLAIN LAUGH. NICE TOUCH.
WRRRRRRRR
TACTACTACTACTAC
IT'S MAGNIFICENT! SO MUCH RAW POWER!
BUT IT'S BUILDING TO CRITICAL MASS!
IT'S GOING TO--IT'S GOING TO GO--

KABOOOOOM
OOOOH...
THE ENERGY... WAS TOO... GREAT...
IT BLEW OUT THE WALL...
BUT WHAT ABOUT THE DOG AND THOSE TWO CATS?

NOW.
MEOWWWRRRRRR
GGRRWWLLL
ATTENTION, ALL UNITS! ALL UNITS RESPOND!
WE HAVE REPORTS OF TWO...UH...GIANT CREATURES IN THE WAREHOUSE DISTRICT...
THEY ARE DESCRIBED AS A BIG ORANGE TABBY CAT AND A BIG YELLOW DOG...
ATTENTION ALL UNITS! THIS IS NOT A JOKE! WE REPEAT, THIS IS NOT A JOKE.

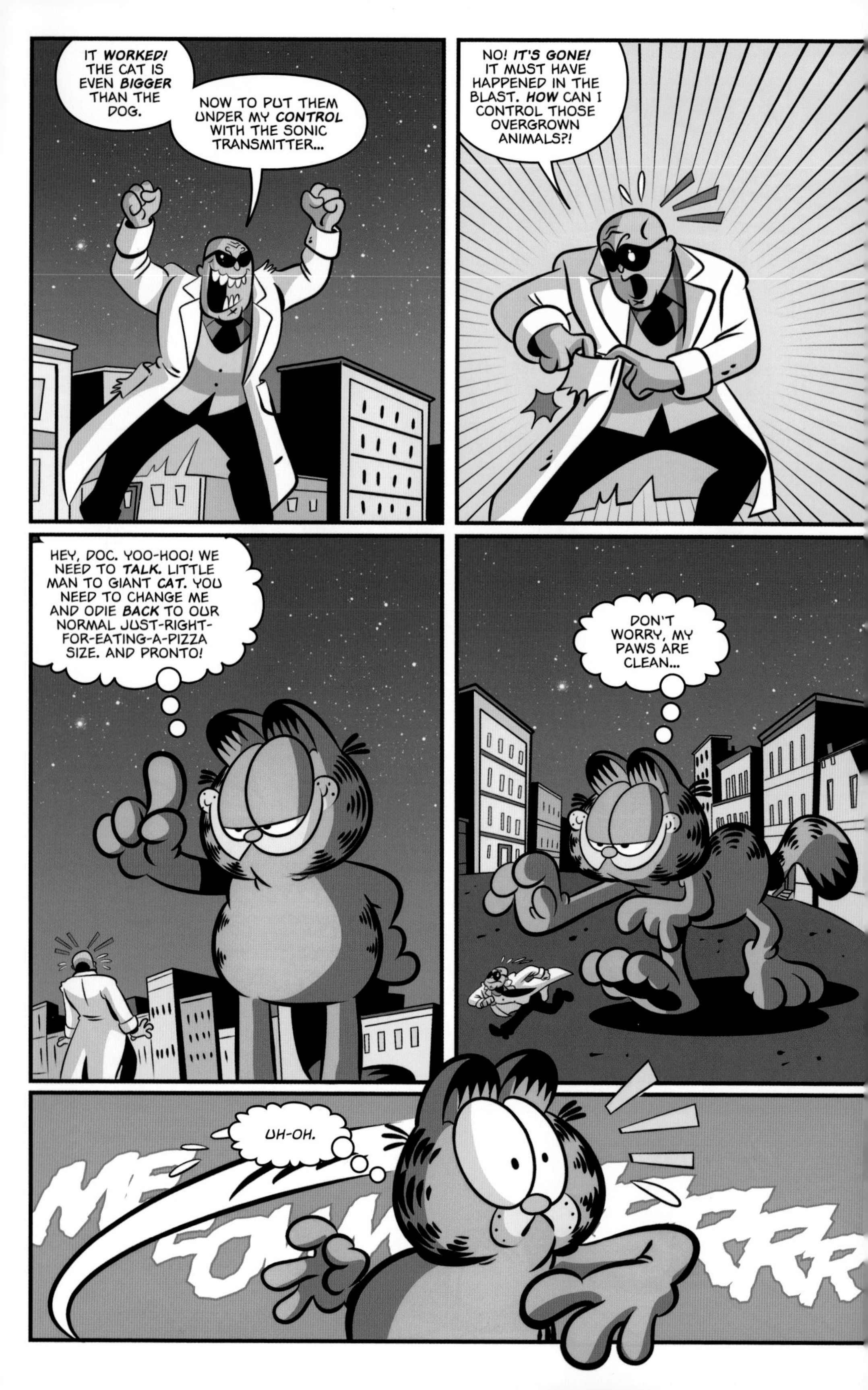
IT WORKED! THE CAT IS EVEN BIGGER THAN THE DOG.
NOW TO PUT THEM UNDER MY CONTROL WITH THE SONIC TRANSMITTER...
NO! IT'S GONE! IT MUST HAVE HAPPENED IN THE BLAST. HOW CAN I CONTROL THOSE OVERGROWN ANIMALS?!
HEY, DOC. YOO-HOO! WE NEED TO TALK. LITTLE MAN TO GIANT CAT. YOU NEED TO CHANGE ME AND ODIE BACK TO OUR NORMAL JUST-RIGHT-FOR-EATING-A-PIZZA SIZE. AND PRONTO!
DON'T WORRY, MY PAWS ARE CLEAN...
UH-OH.

BRA-KOOOOM
MEEEOOWWRRRRRR
LOUIE? HANG ON, BIG FELLA. I'M NOT THE ENEMY HERE.

HISSSSSS
OOF!
CRASH
GRRRRRR
ARGH! YA STUPID MUTT!
WHAMMO
GET OFF MY BACK!
LOUIE KNOWS JUDO? THAT CAT IS FULL OF SURPRISES!

COME ON, GUYS! IT'S OUR CHANCE TO *ESCAPE!*
SQUEAK SQUEAK
YES! SWEET *FREEDOM!*
I SAY! GOOD SHOW!
HEY, GUYS! LOOK! *FOOD!*
A FREE *BUFFET!* LET'S CHOW DOWN!
X95-43J PROTEIN
PET FOOD
MUNCH
MUNCH
MUNCH
PECK PECK
PECK PECK

CLICK
CLICK
WRRRRRRRRR
TACTACTACTACTAC
OOH, PARTY LIGHTS. LET'S DANCE, BABY!
TACTACTACTACTAC
SQUEAK SQUEAK
TACTACTACTAC
MY WORD! WE'RE IN A BIT OF A PICKLE!
I DARE NOT OPEN MY EYES!
♬♫♫♫
TAC
TACTACTAC

HEY, WHAT WAS IN THAT FOOD?
SQUEAK SQUEAK
WE'RE ALL HUGE! I THINK I'LL FIND A HUMAN AND MAKE HIM MY PET! HEE-HEE!
MOMMY, I WISH I HAD A GIANT PET LIKE THAT BIG DOG AND CAT.
MAYBE A HAMSTER!
SQUEAK SQUEAK
WHEEEEEE!
BILLY! DON'T!
YEE-HAW!
BILLY! COME BACK! BILLY!

I SAY, NIGEL. I DO WE BELIEVE WE'VE CAUSED A BIT OF A FENDER BENDER.
RATHER! I HOPE THEY'RE INSURED BY TH COMPANY THAT EMPLOY THAT CUTE LITTLE GECKO.
GET OUT OF HERE, YOU STUPID BIRDS!
PLOP
MMMPHHRR!

M GONNA ENJOY TAKING U DOWN, TUBBY. A HOUSE AT LIKE YOU IS NO MATCH FOR A GUY FROM THE STREETS.
IF YOU MEAN THAT TERRIBLE BODY ODOR, YOU'RE RIGHT. YOU STINK LIKE AN OLD LITTER BOX!
DIDN'T THINK I'D BE THAT QUICK, DID YOU?
ACTUALLY, I DIDN'T THINK SO, EITHER.
LUCKILY, I'VE SPENT A LOT OF TIME WATCHING PROFESSIONAL WRESTLING ON TV, AND I'VE PICKED UP A FEW MOVES...
HEY!
ET'S START WITH THE CHICKENWING...
OWWW!
THEN ON TO A CAMEL CLUTCH...
OW! OW! I'M GONNA GET YOU, CAT...

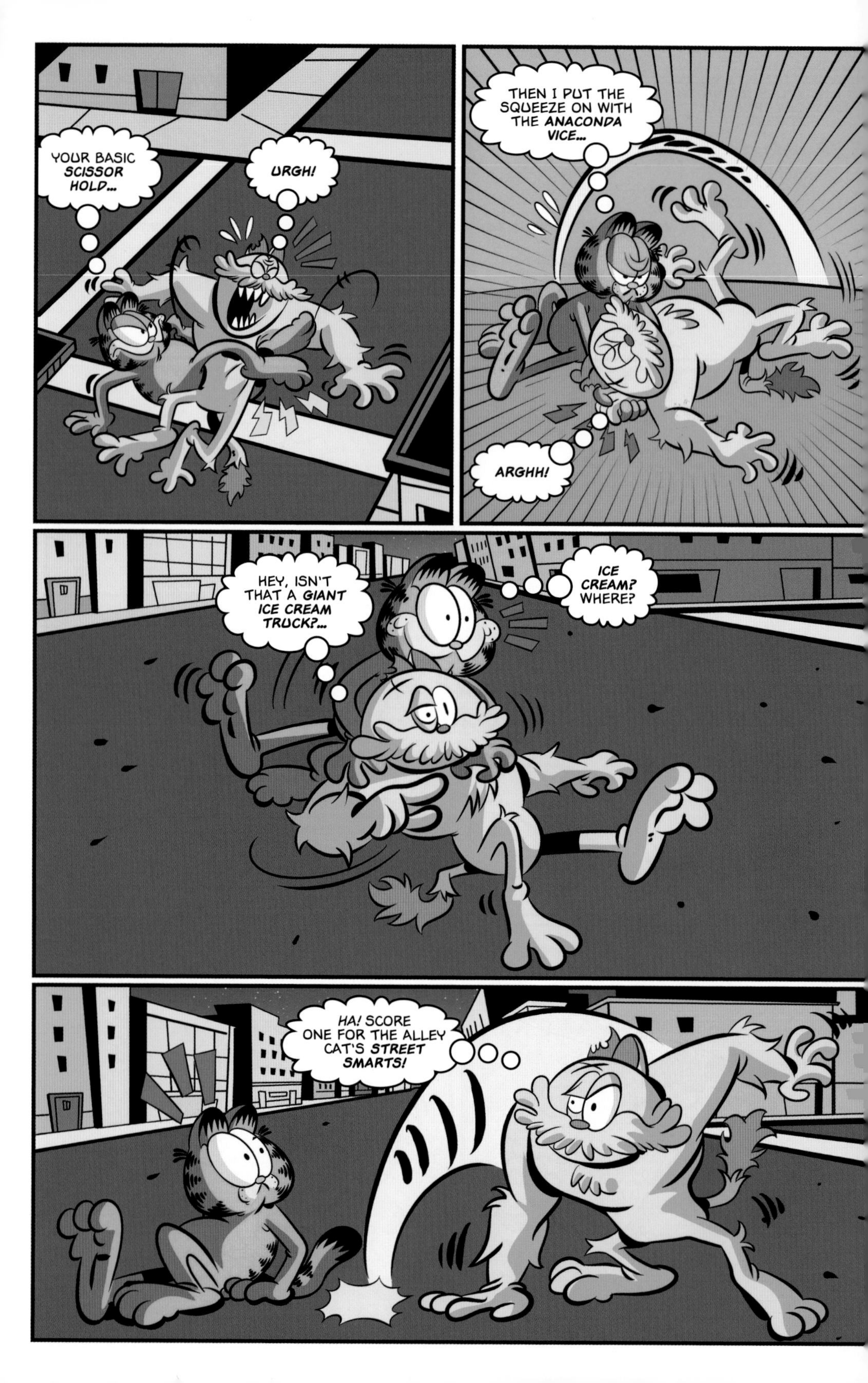
YOUR BASIC SCISSOR HOLD...
URGH!
THEN I PUT THE SQUEEZE ON WITH THE ANACONDA VICE...
ARGHH!
HEY, ISN'T THAT A GIANT ICE CREAM TRUCK?...
ICE CREAM? WHERE?
HA! SCORE ONE FOR THE ALLEY CAT'S STREET SMARTS!

OME ON, LOUIE...
WHADDAYA SAY WE STOP ALL THIS FIGHTING? I'M WORKING UP A SWEAT, AND I REALLY HATE TO SWEAT. I'M GENERALLY ALLERGIC TO EXERCISE. AND MORNINGS, AND--
RIIPPPP
ONUTS.
YAK, YAK, YAK! YOU SURE LIKE TO TALK, DON'T YOU, HOUSE CAT?
WELL, MAYBE THIS WILL SHUT YOU UP!
SLAMM
MMMPHH!
PTOOEY
OKAY, NOW I'M MAD.

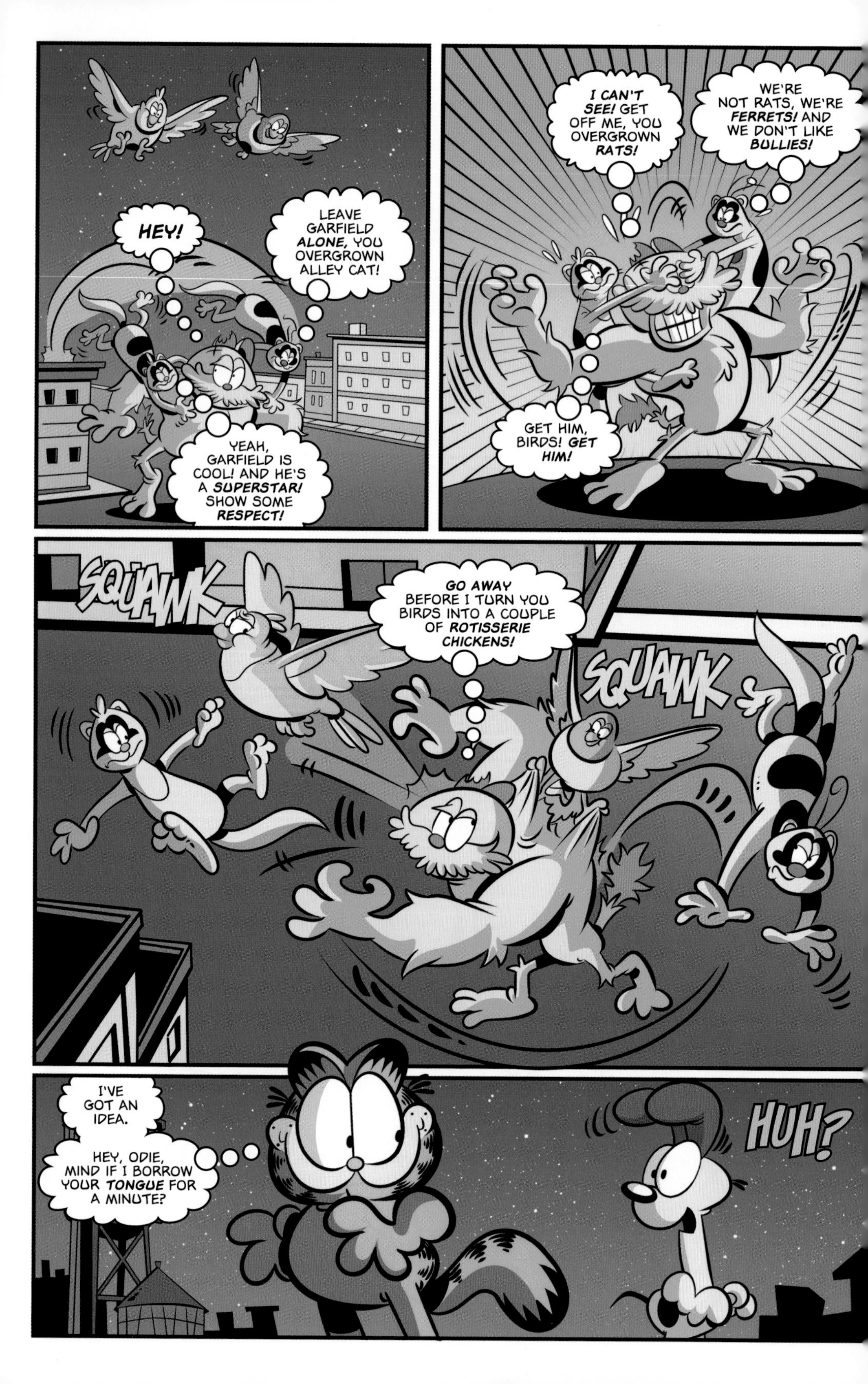
HEY!
LEAVE GARFIELD ALONE, YOU OVERGROWN ALLEY CAT!
YEAH, GARFIELD IS COOL! AND HE'S A SUPERSTAR! SHOW SOME RESPECT!
I CAN'T SEE! GET OFF ME, YOU OVERGROWN RATS!
WE'RE NOT RATS, WE'RE FERRETS! AND WE DON'T LIKE BULLIES!
GET HIM, BIRDS! GET HIM!
SQUAWK
GO AWAY BEFORE I TURN YOU BIRDS INTO A COUPLE OF ROTISSERIE CHICKENS!
SQUAWK
I'VE GOT AN IDEA.
HEY, ODIE, MIND IF I BORROW YOUR TONGUE FOR A MINUTE?
HUH?

DON'T TRY THIS AT HOME. ODIE IS A PROFESSIONAL CARTOON DOG WITH A SUPER-STRETCHY CARTOON TONGUE.
STRETCH
STRETCH
STRETCH
OKAY, I'VE HOG TIED HIM--OR RATHER, DOG TIED HIM.
NOW WHAT?
ARGH! LET ME GO!

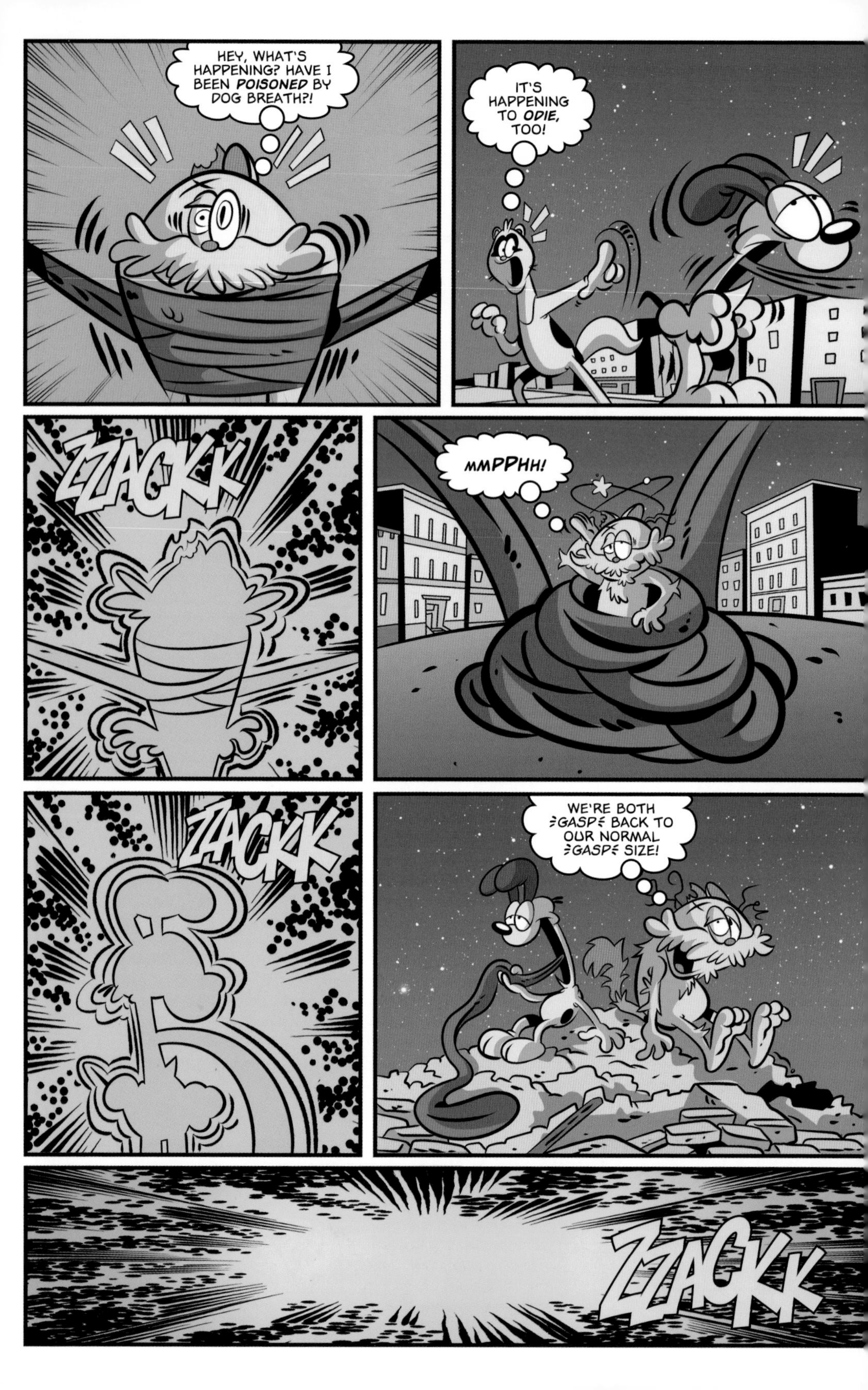
HEY, WHAT'S HAPPENING? HAVE I BEEN POISONED BY DOG BREATH?!
IT'S HAPPENING TO ODIE, TOO!
ZZACKK
MMPPHH!
ZZACKK
WE'RE BOTH ≷GASP≶ BACK TO OUR NORMAL ≷GASP≶ SIZE!
ZZACKK

THE EFFECTS OF THE RAYGUN THINGY ARE ONLY TEMPORARY, I GUESS.
THAT'S A RELIEF! (AND A CONVENIENT WAY TO WRAP UP THIS STORY, TOO!)
LOOKS LIKE YOU PET SHOP BOYS AND GIRLS WILL STAY BIGGER FOR A WHILE LONGER.
CAN I HAVE YOUR AUTOGRAPH, GARFIELD? I'M YOUR BIGGEST FAN.
YOU CERTAINLY ARE!
WE JUST NEED TO WRAP UP A LOOSE END, FIRST.
HEY, BIRDY! I HAVE A FAVOR TO ASK!
THIS DIDN'T GO QUITE AS PLANNED. BUT I'VE GOT MY PASSPORT AND BOOKED A TICKET ON A CRUISE TO BELIZE.
SOON I'LL BE SAFELY OUT OF THE COUNTRY!
WHAT?!
NO! STOP! I'M AFRAID OF FLYING!

DROP
?!
DR. NIEMANN!
OFFICERS, I THINK WE'VE JUST FOUND WHO'S RESPONSIBLE FOR THIS OVERSIZED MESS.
DR. NIEMANN MUST HAVE STOLEN MY REJUVENATING PROTEIN COMPOUND AND COMBINED IT WITH COSMIC RAYS TO INCREASE THE ANIMALS' SIZES.
WE'RE FORTUNATE THE EFFECTS DIDN'T LAST LONG.
I HAVE ONLY ONE THING TO SAY: LAWYER! LAWYER!
I'M COVERED IN DOG SPIT. YUCK!
I'D FEEL SORRY FOR YOU IF IT WASN'T FOR THAT WHOLE CRAMMING-A-GIANT-FIBERGLASS-DONUT-IN-MY-MOUTH THING.
BUT I GUESS EVERYTHING'S NORMAL AGAIN...
SPLOT
OR IT WILL BE, ONCE THOSE GIANT BIRDS GO BACK TO THEIR REGULAR SIZE!
RUN!
—THE END—

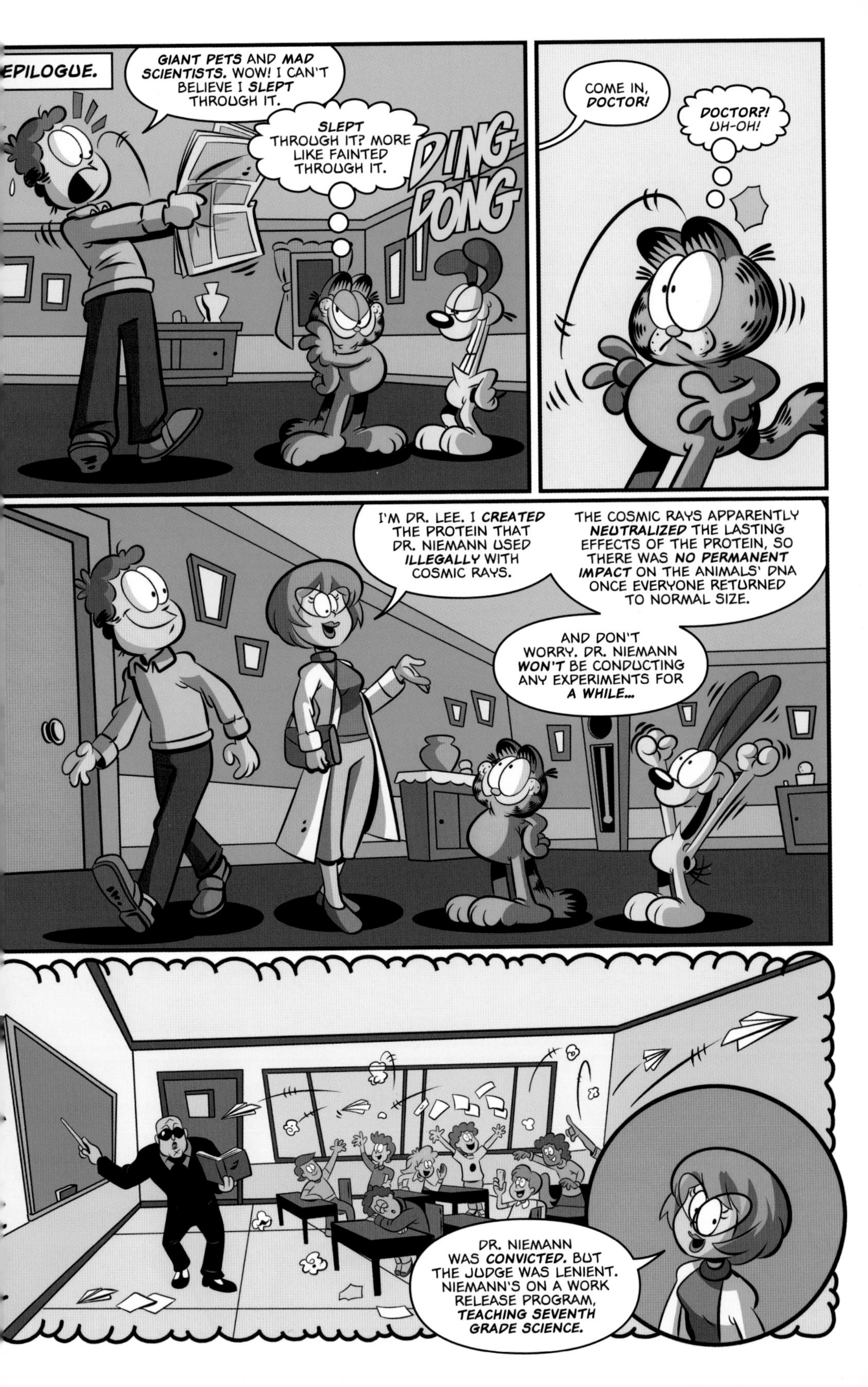
EPILOGUE.
GIANT PETS AND MAD SCIENTISTS. WOW! I CAN'T BELIEVE I SLEPT THROUGH IT.
SLEPT THROUGH IT? MORE LIKE FAINTED THROUGH IT.
DING DONG
COME IN, DOCTOR!
DOCTOR?! UH-OH!
I'M DR. LEE. I CREATED THE PROTEIN THAT DR. NIEMANN USED ILLEGALLY WITH COSMIC RAYS.
THE COSMIC RAYS APPARENTLY NEUTRALIZED THE LASTING EFFECTS OF THE PROTEIN, SO THERE WAS NO PERMANENT IMPACT ON THE ANIMALS' DNA ONCE EVERYONE RETURNED TO NORMAL SIZE.
AND DON'T WORRY. DR. NIEMANN WON'T BE CONDUCTING ANY EXPERIMENTS FOR A WHILE...
DR. NIEMANN WAS CONVICTED. BUT THE JUDGE WAS LENIENT. NIEMANN'S ON A WORK RELEASE PROGRAM, TEACHING SEVENTH GRADE SCIENCE.

HA! THAT SOUNDS LIKE CRUEL AND UNUSUAL PUNISHMENT TO ME.
I DISMANTLED NIEMANN'S COSMIC RAY GUN. BUT BEFORE I DID, I USED IT ONE LAST TIME...
YOUR OWNER TOLD ME HOW MUCH YOU LIKED DONUTS!
SWEET!
NOW I JUST NEED FORTY GALLONS OF COFFEE!
THE END

"THE GOLDEN MACGUFFIN"

THE OFFICE SMELLED LIKE CHEAP CIGARS AND EVEN CHEAPER PIZZA.
I WAS "BETWEEN ASSIGNMENTS," AS WE SAY IN THE BUSINESS, AND MY WALLET WAS A LITTLE LIGHT, SO INSTEAD OF ONE OF VITO'S SUPREME PIZZAS WITH EXTRA PEPPERONI, SAUSAGE, CHEESE AND ANCHOVIES, I HAD TO SETTLE FOR A SMALL THIN CRUST PIE FROM PIZZA WORLD THAT TASTED LIKE WARMED-UP CARDBOARD.
THE NAME ON THE DOOR READ "SAM SPAYED, PRIVATE INVESTIGATOR." ACTUALLY, THE NAME ON THE DOOR READ "IRVING ROTH, ACCOUNTANT." I'D MOVED TO MY NEW, SMALLER, SMELLIER AND LESS EXPENSIVE OFFICE TWO WEEKS AGO BUT HADN'T GOTTEN AROUND TO CHANGING THE MONIKER. SIGN PAINTERS, LIKE GOOD PIZZA, COST MONEY AND THAT WAS SOMETHING I WAS IN SHORT SUPPLY OF.
I'D TAPED A SHEET OF PAPER WITH MY NAME ON THE GLASS. IT WASN'T FANCY, OR PROFESSIONAL, BUT IT GOT THE JOB DONE.
I WAS JUST ABOUT TO HAVE MY FIFTH CUP OF COFFEE WHEN I HEARD AN URGENT KNOCK ON THE DOOR.
IRVING ROTH
ACCOUNTANT
KNOCK! KNOCK! KNOCK!
EXTRA
THE GOLDEN MACGUFFIN

IS THIS THE OFFICE OF SAM SPAYED?
THAT'S WHAT THE DOOR SAYS.
ACTUALLY THE DOOR SAYS IRVING ROTH, ACCOUNTANT...
Irving Roth Accountant
WELL, THAT'S WHAT THE PAPER TAPED TO THE DOOR SAYS.
WHAT CAN I DO FOR YOU?
SAM SPAYED DETECTIVE
I NEED YOUR HELP, MR. SPAYED.
MY NAME IS GLORIA DEAN, AND I THINK MY LIFE IS IN DANGER.
"LAST NIGHT, SOMEONE TRIED TO RUN ME OVER...
"TOSSED A KNIFE AT ME...
"AND ALMOST DROPPED A SAFE ON MY HEAD!"

THAT SOUNDS VERY SERIOUS. ACTUALLY IT SOUNDS VERY CARTOONY, BUT, YOU KNOW, IN A SERIOUS INJURY WAY.
I THINK THEY'RE AFTER THIS. I INHERITED IT FROM MY GRANDMOTHER JUST LAST WEEK, WHEN SHE PASSED AWAY.
IT'S THE GOLDEN MACGUFFIN, AND IT'S A PRICELESS STATUE!
A MACGUFFIN?
YES, IT'S AN EXTINCT BIRD SIMILAR TO A PENGUIN. ANGUS MACGUFFIN DISCOVERED THE BIRD WHILE EXPLORING THE NORTH POLE.
THANKS FOR THE NATURE LESSON. SO WHAT MAKES THIS GOLDEN MACGUFFIN SO PRICELESS? IS IT FILLED WITH DIAMONDS OR SOMETHING?
NO, EVEN MORE VALUABLE. MY GRANDMOTHER'S CHOCOLATE CHIP COOKIE RECIPE.
THERE ARE THOSE WHO WOULD KILL FOR THAT RECIPE!
MUST BE SOME REALLY GOOD COOKIES.
OH, THEY ARE. THE SECRET IS THE WALNUTS.
CAN I LEAVE THE STATUE WITH YOU FOR SAFEKEEPING WHILE I PACK A BAG? I'M LEAVING ON A BOAT FOR EUROPE THIS AFTERNOON. I'LL BE SAFE OVER THERE.
SO I GET TO BABYSIT GRANNY'S PRICELESS RECIPE?!
SORRY, THIS SOUNDS A LITTLE FISHY. WHY SHOULD I RISK MY LIFE OVER THIS BIRD?
I HAVE CASH. LOTS OF CASH.
LOOKS LIKE I HAVE OVER TWO HUNDRED GOOD REASONS TO WATCH OUR LITTLE GOLDEN FRIEND.

GOOD! I'LL BE BACK IN TWO HOURS.
WHAT'S THIS? A BUSINESS CARD?
Irving Roth Accountant
SLAM
KNOCK! KNOCK! KNOCK!
DID YOU FORGET SOMETHING, MISS...?
ALL RIGHT, GUMSHOE...!
WHERE IS IT? WHERE IS IT?!
I KNOW YOU HAVE IT, SPAYED. I WATCHED HER LEAVE!
SMASH!
WHERE'S THE BIRD? WHERE'S THE MACGUFFIN?
RIGHT ON MY DESK, LUNKHEAD. YOU DIDN'T HAVE TO TRASH MY OFFICE.

WHAM!
NOW FOR THE PRIZE INSIDE!
HEY, WHAT'S THIS? WHERE'S THE PRICELESS JEWELS?
SORRY, SUCKERS!
JEWELS? DIDN'T THE LADY SAY THERE WAS A RECIPE INSIDE THAT STATUE?
LOOKS LIKE YOU'VE BEEN PLAYED. LOOKS LIKE I HAVE, TOO. NOW RUN ALONG BEFORE I CALL THE COPS.
I'M GOING, SPAYED. BUT I'LL FIND THAT LADY AND THE REAL STATUE!
THAT'S JUST WHAT I WAS PLANNING TO DO MYSELF.

I TOOK A CAB TO THE ADDRESS ON THE BUSINESS CARD MISS DEAN DROPPED. IT WAS THE SITE OF THE PURPLE PAGODA, A CHINESE RESTAURANT THAT CLOSED DOWN AFTER A FIRE. A DEAD END.
AN INTENSE CRAVING FOR MOO SHU SHRIMP HIT ME LIKE A WAVE. I WAS STARVING, BUT WHAT I REALLY WANTED WAS A PIZZA FROM VITO'S, AND I NOW HAD A POCKET FULL FRESH CASH TO HELP ME.
THE PURPLE PAGODA.
CLOSED
I WALKED THE SIX BLOCKS TO VITO'S, MY STOMACH RUMBLING LIKE FREIGHT TRAIN.
ALL THE WAY I KEPT THINKING: WHAT DID THE BUSINESS CARD MEAN AND WHY DID THE LADY CONVENIENTLY DROP IT? AND WHEN WERE THEY GOING TO REOPEN THE PURPLE PAGODA? AND WHEN THEY DID, WOULD THEY HAVE MOO SHU SHRIMP ON THE MENU?
VITO
VITO
HI, GUIDO. GIVE ME A VITO'S SUPREME--A LARGE WITH EXTRA PEPPERONI, SAUSAGE, CHEESE AND ANCHOVIES. DOUBLE ORDER OF GARLIC BREAD WITH CHEESE, CAESAR SALAD, VEAL PARMESAN AND TIRAMISU FOR DESSERT!

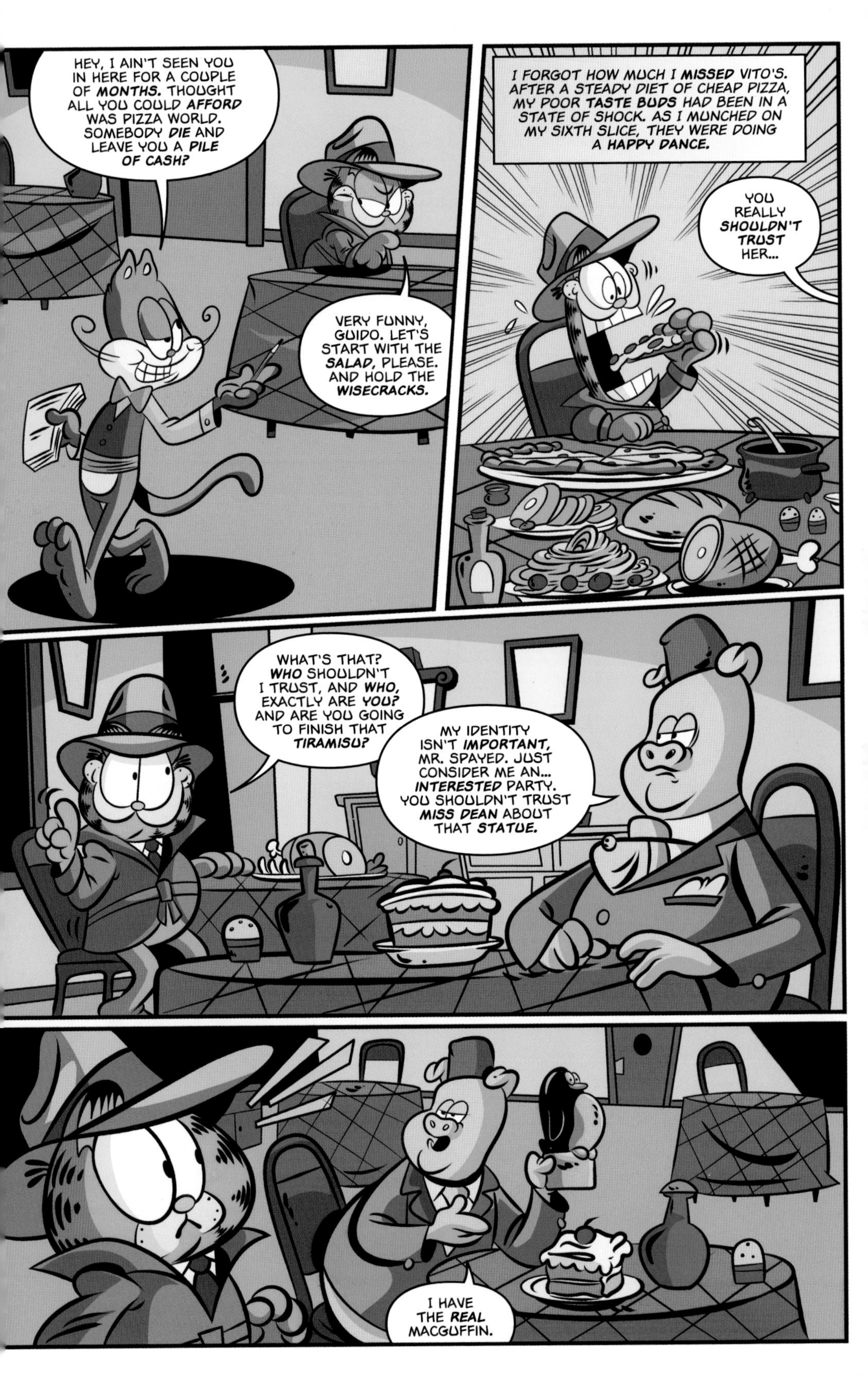
HEY, I AIN'T SEEN YOU IN HERE FOR A COUPLE OF MONTHS. THOUGHT ALL YOU COULD AFFORD WAS PIZZA WORLD. SOMEBODY DIE AND LEAVE YOU A PILE OF CASH?
VERY FUNNY, GUIDO. LET'S START WITH THE SALAD, PLEASE. AND HOLD THE WISECRACKS.
I FORGOT HOW MUCH I MISSED VITO'S. AFTER A STEADY DIET OF CHEAP PIZZA, MY POOR TASTE BUDS HAD BEEN IN A STATE OF SHOCK. AS I MUNCHED ON MY SIXTH SLICE, THEY WERE DOING A HAPPY DANCE.
YOU REALLY SHOULDN'T TRUST HER...
WHAT'S THAT? WHO SHOULDN'T I TRUST, AND WHO, EXACTLY ARE YOU? AND ARE YOU GOING TO FINISH THAT TIRAMISU?
MY IDENTITY ISN'T IMPORTANT, MR. SPAYED. JUST CONSIDER ME AN... INTERESTED PARTY. YOU SHOULDN'T TRUST MISS DEAN ABOUT THAT STATUE.
I HAVE THE REAL MACGUFFIN.

OKAY, SPAYED. HERE'S THE CHECK.
THANKS, GUIDO. KEEP THE CHANGE.
NOW BACK TO THE MATTER AT HAND, TUBBY. HOW DO I KNOW YOUR MACGUFFIN ISN'T ANOTHER FAKE?
HEY, WHAT GIVES, SPAYED?
TWENTY BUCKS!!!
THIS BILL IS PHONY! WHAT ARE YOU TRYIN' TO PULL?
HEY, TINY! TAKE CARE OF THIS PUNK!
TINY?

THROW THIS BUM OUT. HE WAS TRYING TO PASS SOME BAD CABBAGE!
HELLO, TINY. OBVIOUSLY YOU ARE NAMED IRONICALLY.
TAKE YOUR WISECRACKS AND YOUR FUNNY MONEY SOMEPLACE ELSE!
TOSS!
OOF!
A FAKE BIRD, A FAKE ADDRESS AND FAKE MONEY. WHAT KIND OF SCHEME WAS MISS DEAN, MY FELINE FEMME FATALE, PULLING?
AND HOW DID THAT BIG PIG'S MACGUFFIN FIGURE INTO IT?
AND MOST IMPORTANT, WHY DIDN'T I GRAB HIS DESSERT BEFORE THEY TOSSED ME OUT?
I NEEDED TO FIND SOME ANSWERS.
SO I DECIDED TO HIT UP ALL THE USUAL SUSPECTS, ASKING IF THEY HAD ANY INFORMATION ABOUT THE LADY AND HER MYSTERIOUS GOLDEN STATUE...

MY FIRST STOP WAS "CATNIP" CARL.
THE LAST COUPLE OF DAYS ARE KINDA HAZY, IF YOU KNOW WHAT I MEAN...
THEN "TUNA BREATH" McGEE...
DOESN'T RING A BELL. OF COURSE A FRESH CAN OF ALBACORE MIGHT HELP JOG MY MEMORY...
NATASHA...
I KNOW NOTHING OF THIS MACGUFFIN. AND IF SOMEONE WAS POISONED, IT WAS NOT ME.
"PORKY" JOE...
HEY, I DON'T SQUEAL ON NOBODY...
"ONE-EYED" JACK...
I AIN'T SEEN NOTHIN'!
AND FINALLY, "HAIRBALL" HARRY...
HACK
HACK
HACK
HACK
54

WELL, THAT PROVED TO BE A COLOSSAL WASTE OF TIME. I NEEDED TO FIND A BETTER GROUP OF INFORMANTS.
I DECIDED TO HEAD TO THE DOCKS WHERE THE CRUISE SHIP WAS LEAVING FROM.
THERE SHE WAS! GLORIA DEAN BOARDING THE SHIP. I HAD TO FOLLOW HER.
THIS IS WHAT WE CALL IN THE BUSINESS "SNEAKING ONBOARD"...
HOLD IT RIGHT THERE, PAL!
NO STOWAWAYS ON THIS VOYAGE. SCRAM!
AND THIS IS WHAT WE CALL IN THE BUSINESS "GETTING THROWN OFF"...
SPLASH
I WASN'T EXPECTING AN IMPROMPTU BATH, BUT WHEN I REACHED UP AND FOUND THE SIDE OF THE LIFEBOAT, I WAS IN FOR AN EVEN BIGGER SURPRISE...

YOU?!
I'M SORRY, MR. SPAYED...
THERE WERE CROOKS ON THE SHIP WHO WANTED TO STEAL MY STATUE.
I HAD TO SNEAK OFF IN THIS LIFEBOAT.
OKAY, SISTER, SPILL IT.
WHY DID YOU GIVE ME A FAKE MACGUFFIN TO PROTECT? AND WHAT'S REALLY INSIDE THAT BIRD? IF THAT IS THE REAL BIRD.
ALL RIGHT, I'LL TELL YOU THE TRUTH. THE MACGUFFIN DOESN'T CONTAIN MY GRANDMA'S SECRET RECIPE FOR CHOCOLATE CHIP COOKIES.
IT CONTAINS NATION
SECURITY SECRETS
MICROFILM.
WHAT?
DO NOT ATTEMPT TO ESCAPE!
VROOOM!
I AM WERNER VON WERNER, FOREIGN SPY! I WILL TAKE THAT STATUE. AND ITS TOP-SECRET CONTENTS!

CRACK
WHAT? I HAVE BEEN DOUBLE-CROSSED.
DOUBLE-DOUBLE-CROSSED, ACTUALLY!
HA! HA! HA! YOU'VE BEEN TRIPLE-DOUBLE-CROSSED!
I AM NOT GLORIA DEAN. I AM PATCHY LE FEVER, INTERNATIONAL PIRATE.
"I TIED UP GLORIA AND PUT THE MACGUFFIN IN A SAFE PLACE. WHERE, AS WE SPEAK, ONE OF MY LACKEYS IS EN ROUTE TO RETRIEVE IT."
ARGH! I MUST FIND THAT MACGUFFIN! TELL ME WHERE IT IS!
NEVER, YOU SWINE!
I HAVE WAYS OF MAKING YOU TALK. MOST UNPLEASANT WAYS, YOU WILL FIND...
THAT WAS MY CUE TO EXIT...

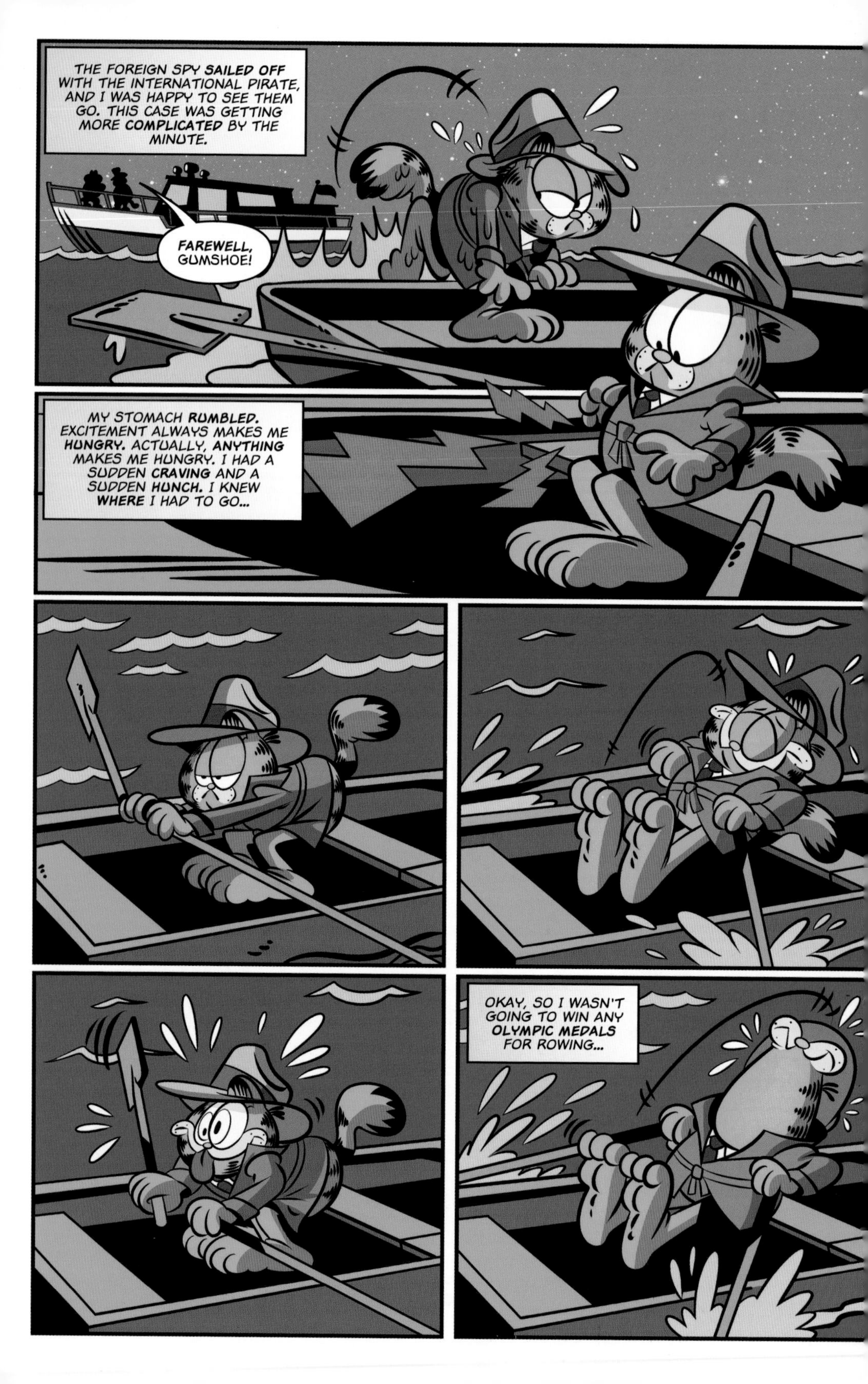
THE FOREIGN SPY SAILED OFF WITH THE INTERNATIONAL PIRATE, AND I WAS HAPPY TO SEE THEM GO. THIS CASE WAS GETTING MORE COMPLICATED BY THE MINUTE.
FAREWELL, GUMSHOE!
MY STOMACH RUMBLED. EXCITEMENT ALWAYS MAKES ME HUNGRY. ACTUALLY, ANYTHING MAKES ME HUNGRY. I HAD A SUDDEN CRAVING AND A SUDDEN HUNCH. I KNEW WHERE I HAD TO GO...
OKAY, SO I WASN'T GOING TO WIN ANY OLYMPIC MEDALS FOR ROWING...

THIRTY-SEVEN EXHAUSTING MINUTES LATER...
...I FINALLY MADE IT TO DOCK.
HEY, CABBIE!
CABBIE, TAKE ME TO THIS ADDRESS. AND STEP ON IT!
SURE THING, MAC.
SAY, AREN'T YOU THAT PRIVATE EYE, NICK NEUTERED? I READ ABOUT YOU IN THE PAPER.
IT'S SPAYED. SAM SPAYED.
SORRY, MAC. MY MISTAKE. YOU MUST LEAD A PRETTY EXCITING LIFE, RIGHT? LOTS OF DAMES AND DANGER...
I PREFER TO SAY "BABES AND BULLETS"...

SAY, WHAT'S THAT?
SOMEONE IS FOLLOWING US.
DO WHAT YOU CAN TO LOSE 'EM!
VROOOM!
HEY! WATCH IT!
SCREECH!
WHOEVER'S DRIVING THAT CAR WANTS ME AND WANTS ME BAD...

I GUESS THAT CABBIE DON'T KNOW THE RULES OF THE ROAD...
ALWAYS YIELD TO THE BIG DOG WITH THE RIGHT OF WAY!
WE GOT SOME UNFINISHED BUSINESS, SPAYED...
SURPRISE, YA BIG LUG!
WHY THAT ROTTEN, NO-GOOD CAT...
THAT'S WHAT WE PRIVATE INVESTIGATORS CALL "THE OL' SWITCHEROO."
IF MY HUNCH WAS RIGHT, ONCE I GOT INSIDE THE PLACE I'D FIND...

PURPLE PAGODA
GLORIA DEAN AND THE GOLDEN MACGUFFIN!
SO, LEVEL WITH ME. WHAT'S REALLY INSIDE THAT BIRD? PRECIOUS GEMS, A COOKIE RECIPE OR NATIONAL SECRETS?
HEY, WHAT GIVES?!
CRASH! BANG! CRUNCH!
OUCH! OOF!
SORRY, MR. SPAYED, YOU WON'T FIND THE ANSWER TO THAT QUESTION

THIS BIG GALOOT WON'T BE ANY MORE TROUBLE. HE'S NICELY PACKAGED FOR THE AUTHORITIES... I MUST SAY, MY KNOT-TYING ABILITIES ARE QUITE AMAZING!
OOOH, MY HEAD...
AS FOR MISS DEAN AND THE MACGUFFIN, THEY ARE NO LONGER YOUR CONCERN.
THEY'RE NOT?
BUT DON'T WORRY, THEY'RE SAFE WITH ME...
BRIDGET O'MALLEY, GOVERNMENT AGENT!
I'M RETURNING THE CONTENTS OF THE MACGUFFIN TO MY SUPERIORS, BUT I LEFT YOU A LITTLE GIFT. SOMETHING TO REMEMBER US BY...

SO WHAT DID THE THE GOVERNMENT AGENT LEAVE ME, YOU MAY ASK?
FIVE THOUSAND BUCKS. NOT A BAD PAYDAY FOR TIME SPENT. NOW I COULD GET THAT SIGN ON MY DOOR REPAINTED. MAYBE FIX UP THE OFFICE A BIT, TOO.
OH, AND THAT'S NOT ALL.
I ALSO GOT A PLATE OF COOKIES.
KNOCK! KNOCK! KNOCK!
THE BEST CHOCOLATE CHIP COOKIES I HAD EVER EATEN.
THE SECRET WAS THE WALNUTS...
MR. SPAYED! IT'S URGENT THAT I SPEAK WITH YOU. I'M AFRAID YOU'VE BEEN DUPED ONCE MORE!
Irving Roth Accountant
PIGLEY? YOU AGAIN? GET LOST, CHUBBY!
IT'S NOT PIGLEY. IT'S REALLY ME...
GLORIA DEAN! AND I HAVE THE REAL GOLDEN MACGUFFIN!
WHAT THE--?
YOU HAVE TO PROTECT ME, MR. SPAYED!
OKAY, THAT DOES IT. I NEED TO FIND A NEW LINE OF WORK. MAYBE I CAN CHANGE MY NAME TO IRVING ROTH AND BECOME AN ACCOUNTANT...
THE END

"I HATE MOONDAYS"

WAS NO OG THAT BIT YOU
'TWAS A WOLF
AND 'TWAS NO ORDINARY WOLF
'TWAS A WERE WOLF
AND WITH THE FULL MOON
YOU TOO WILL BECOME A WOLF
VERYTHING OU HOLD DEAR
EVERY PERSON YOU KNOW IS IN GRAVE DANGER
LOCK YOURSELF AWAY
YOU MUST
ME?
A WEREWOLF
HA
SURE THING, GRANDMA
UH OH
I'VE GOT A BAD FEELING ABOUT THIS, POOKY
FOOL!
HEED MY WARNING
BEWARE! BEWAAAARE!

HA HA
CAN YOU BELIEVE THAT OLD CRONE?
WHAT A LOON
OH WOW
WOULDJA LOOK AT THAT BIG BEAUTIFUL MOON
GIK
I DON'T FEEL SO GOOD
I FEEL
I FEEL
WHAT IS IT DEAR?
DARLING, ARE YOU OKAY?
GRRRRRRREAT
AAAAA AAAAA AAAAA
WELP
THAT'S ENOUGH TV FOR TONIGHT, POOKY
CLIK

Z
YIP
YIPYIP
Z
BOY, LIZ, IT'S REALLY STARTING TO COME DOWN OUT THERE
OH IT'S NOTHING TO WORRY ABOUT
YEAH IT WAS SOME BIG WEIRD DOG AT THE PARK
IT'S JUST A SCRATCH. IT'S FINE!

IT CAME OUT OF THE BUSHES AND BIT ME, AND THEN IT JUST RAN OFF INTO THE WOODS
SO BATTEN DOWN THE HATCHES, FOLKS, WE'RE IN FOR A ROUGH ONE, TONIGHT
WE'RE TALKING WEATHER NOT F FOR MAN NOR BEAST, CHUCK
CLIK
NOR MANBEAST, DALE, IF WE'VE GOT ANY WERE-WOLVES OUT THER IN THE VIEWING AREA HA HA
IT IS A FULL MOON, TONIGHT
UH OH
AWOOOO HA HA
YIP
GAH ODIE
HEY, UH
ODIE, LISTEN
THIS DOG THAT BIT JON
AWOOOOOOOO
A WOLF?!

ODIE, I THINK JON COULD BE--
WE NOW RETURN TO "BINKY THE CLOWN VS. WOLFMAN"
HEEEEEEYYY KID
WE'RE NOT O DIFFERENT, YOU AND I
YOU, WITH YOUR LYCANTHROPY
SPLUT
AND ME
I LIKE AND THROW PIES
TOMATO, TOMAHTO
POTATO, POTAHAAAAAAAAAAAAAAAAAA
I THINK JON MIGHT BE
ONE OF THOSE

SURE HE'S JON ARBUCKLE NOW, BUT ONCE HE TRANSFORMS HE'LL BE A HORRIBLE BEAST
THE FULL MOON'S **TONIGHT**

NOBODY'LL BE SAFE

THINK OF ARLENE, ODIE
THINK OF POOKY
THINK OF NERMAL

OKAY WELL MAYBE NOT NERMAL
BUT THINK OF **JON**
AND WHAT THE WORLD WOULD DO TO JON ARBUCKLE IF THEY FIND OUT HE'S A WEREWOLF
THINK ABOUT WHAT THE WORL DOES TO JON ARBUCKLE WHE HE'S **NOT** A WEREWOLF
DON'T WORRY, BOY
I'VE GOT A PLAN
NOW

"WHERE'S JON?"
LA DONNA È MOBILE

PERFECT
I'M GONNA NEED YOUR LEASH
AND JON'S UMBRELLA
BOOM
SQUEEP
SQUEEP
HMM
LET'S SEE
FOLLICOOL
Whisker Whisperer
HUH
HAIRDY HAIR HAIR
DR. LUMBER JACK
HIRSUTE YOURSELF
HAVEN'T TRIED THIS ONE YET
OH JON
YOU LOOK SO RUGGED
BLUP
OH
"USE SPARINGLY"
WHOOPS
WELL, PROBABLY WON'T MATTER ANYWAY

BRUSH
BRUSH

BOOM

SIGH
BRUSH
BRUSH
BRUSH

WELL, ODIE
AT LEAST IT'S STOPPED RAINING?

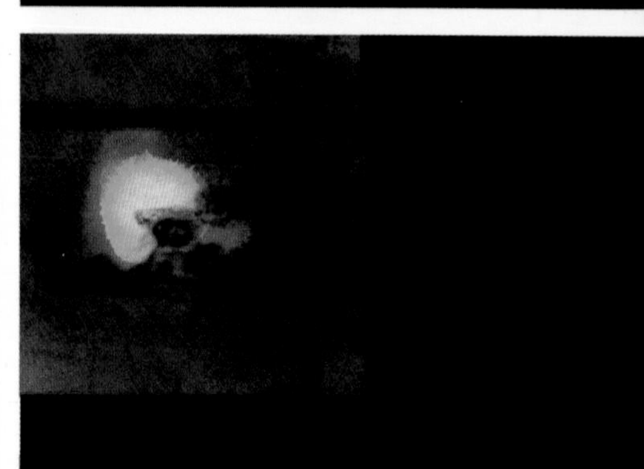

CLICK

HA HA!
WAIT'LL THE BOYS SEE THIS
UGH
THE HUMIDITY MUST'VE SWELLED THE DOORJAMB
CHOOKA CHOOKA CHOOKA
CHOOKA CHOOKA CHOOKA
RRRRRR RRGHHHH
CHOOKA CHOOKA CHOOKA
GIMME A HAND, ODIE
ATTABOY
CHOMP
RATS

GRRR!
PIP
YEAAAARRGHH
KLONK
BOY
EVERYONE'S A CRITIC
THE END

Ask a Dog

"DEAR ASK A DOG"...
"DO DOGS REALLY EAT HOMEWORK?"
MUNCH MUNCH MUNCH
JIM DAVIS 1-3
"DEAR ASK A DOG"...
"WOULD YOU PLEASE LEAVE ME ALONE?"
SIGNED, "MISTER TENNIS BALL"
JIM DAVIS 2-8
"DEAR ASK A DOG"...
"GRRRRRR!"
PLEASE, NO HATE MAIL
JIM DAVIS 2-3
"DEAR ASK A DOG,"
"WHY ARE YOU GUYS ALWAYS SMELLING STUFF?"
JUST ANSWER THE QUESTION!
SNIFF SNIFF
JIM DAVIS 1-13
DEAR "ASK A DOG"...
"WHO IS A GOOD LITTLE DOGGIE?! IS IT YOU?! HUH?! HUH?!"
I CAN'T READ ANY MORE OF THIS
JIM DAVIS 7-15

Garfield Goes GREEN
Instead of disposable cups, use a mug.
DONUTS FEAR ME
WAKEY-WAKEY
Trade in your gas guzzler for a hybrid.

Garfield Goes GREEN
Conserve energy. Take a nap.
Z
Use PUBLIC TRANSPORTATION.
ICE CREAM

SIMPLY ODIE
Cute enough for ya?
Keep OFF the GRASS
LIFE IS A WALK IN THE PARK
puppy love

5 THINGS YOU DON'T KNOW ABOUT ODIE THE DOG

Secretly dated Miss Piggy

Briefly worked as Snoopy's stunt double

Campaigned to Stop Global Worming

His drool is an industrial-strength paint remover

Has over 5,000 bones buried in the backyard

Mouse in the House

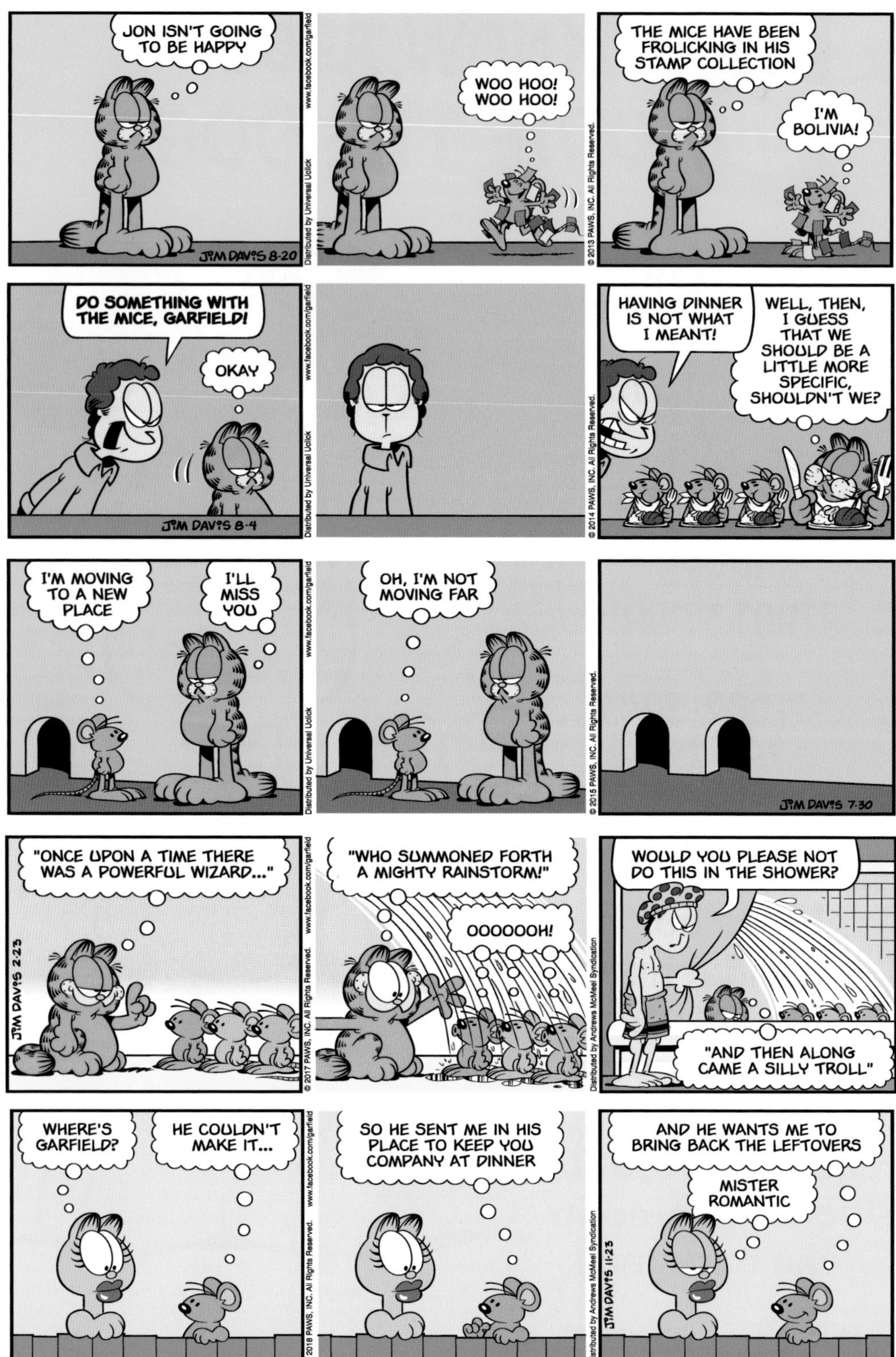

Mouse Party!

Mouse Party!

Garfield Sunday Classics

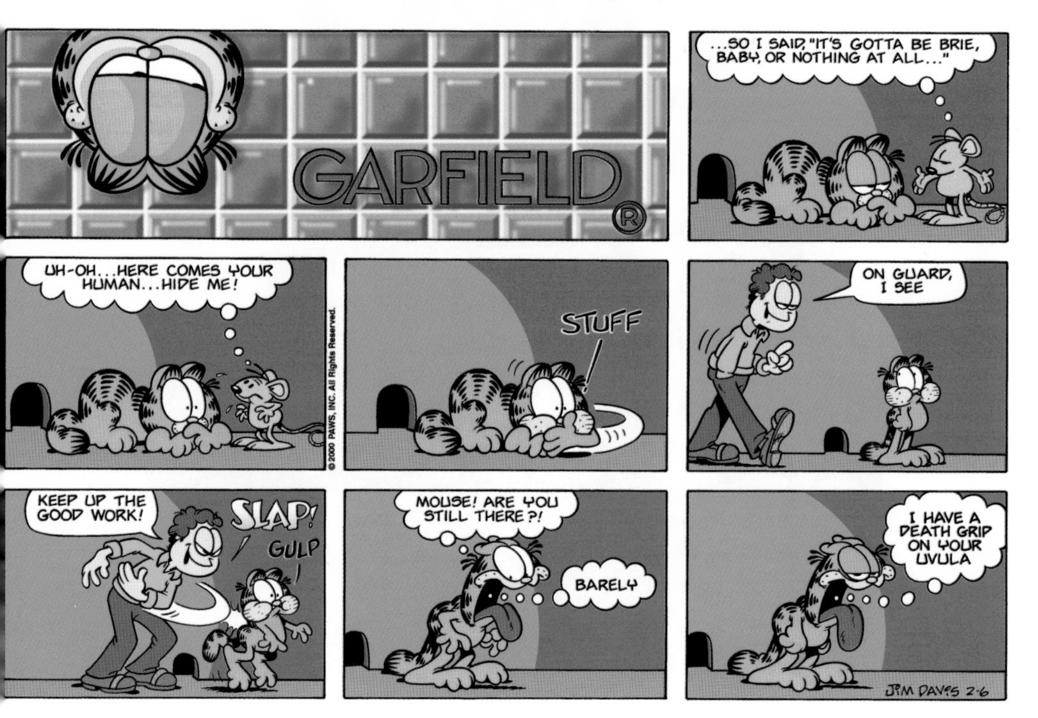

KEEP
YOUR FACE
OUTTA
MY SPACE

ADVENTURE TIME

Sam Sykes • Selina Espiritu • Sarah Stern
Brave Chef Brianna

KELLY THOMPSON BRIANNE DROUHARD M. VICTORIA ROBADO
MEGA PRINCESS

OVER THE GARDEN WALL

STEVEN UNIVERSE
VOLUME ONE

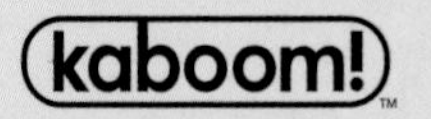
kaboom!